Published by: Next Foundation Press

Text & Cover Design by: Melissa King

Illustrations by: Ricardo Ayala

ISBN-13: 979-8-9890285-0-4

The Raft and the Speedboat

Dr. John A. King

THE RAFT & THE SPEEDBOAT

a short story by:

DR. JOHN A. KING

The old man stood on the boat dock with his grandson, Jack, a passionate, wild-eyed young man in his twenties, looking out over the tranquil hills and valley that surrounded the farm. A stream running between the hills fed the vibrant lake year-round on its way to the ocean many miles away.

Tethered to the dock was a 1948 Chris Craft runabout the old man had painfully restored years ago. Next to it was a six-man inflatable raft similar to the one that the old man's father had used in World War II.

They both stared at the runabout. The boy knew the stories were about to start, and they did. How Granddad

had courted Grandma in it; how all the kids learned to water ski; and the time his sister Bethany won the State Championship.

Jack smiled quietly as Granddad talked, knowing that the only reason he probably didn't sell the boat was that he enjoyed pissing off "all them fancy new neighbors from town who just came up for the weekend, bloody tree huggers." Before she died, his mother said he and his granddad were very much alike, and he was starting to believe she was right.

Jack missed his parents badly—often, especially this year as he headed off to college. He moved in with Granddad the same week the accident happened. Grandma had died the year before, and as he looked back, he realized that living together had probably saved them both.

"What's with the raft, Granddad?" Jack asked.

Taking him by the hand, as if he were still only 8, the old man turned and started leading them back toward the house. "Did I ever tell you about the time your Grandma and I took the river all the way to the coast?"

"You did? That would have been a blast."

The old man nodded, "Now let me think...it was Grandma, Bill and Susan Thomas before they were married, and George and Betty Mueller before they had kids."

They climbed the stairs to the front porch. Granddad adjusted an old quilt pillow on his favorite chair, settled in and packed his pipe. He looked down the grass lawn to the lake and said, "The river was high, and we had a lot of snow that year, and the water was bloody cold. Susie fell in on the second day; she nearly turned blue. We decided we would make camp so Susie could dry her clothes over a fire. To give Susie some privacy, all us boys headed back down the river bank to smoke and have a beer. We were about halfway to where we were gettin', when Bill declared that he forgot his pipe and turned back to go get it."

Suddenly, Granddad rocked back in his chair and started

to laugh, the way an old man laughs when he knows the best part of a familiar story is coming up.

"The rest of us boys had all settled in on some rocks when, suddenly, we hear the girls screaming and yelling like they were under attack. So we jumped up and started running back towards camp. George sprinted way ahead of me, but I was close on his heels. I rounded the bend in the track just in time to see Susie launch out of the bush in nothing but her slacks, holding two socks against her chest. She runs out onto the path like she was being chased by a bear, and BOOM, she runs straight bang into George, knocking him to the ground. Then out of the blue, here comes Bill hurtling down the track, running for his life, yelling, 'I didn't see nuthin!' being chased by your Grandma."

The old man was rocking back and forth in his chair, faster and faster, trying to catch his breath between laughs. He took a deep breath and wiped his eyes and continued.

"When Bill had gone back for his pipe, he tried to be sneaky and get into his tent without disturbing Susie. Well, that didn't work out so well. Apparently, Susie was warming herself by the fire, about to take the last of her clothes off, and she heard something in the bushes."

"She turned around to see Bill sneaking by. She let out this mighty scream. Bill looked up at Susie. Your Grandma looked up and saw Bill standing there, staring at Susie. Grandma figured Billy had come to get an eyeful before the wedding, so she started a-yelling."

"Susie, by this stage, is all worked up and just keeps on screaming and screaming! She bent down, picked up the only bit of clothing not hanging over the fire—two wet socks—and ran straight past Grandma into the bushes at full steam. Billy takes off after Susie yelling, 'I didn't see nothing!' and Grandma, ever the guardian of virtue, turns on her heels and starts running after Billy."

The old man is lost; laughing, crying, re-living, re-smelling, retelling the story, while the boy sits, knowing he is hearing something very special, almost sacred.

"Betty told us later that when Susie screamed, Bill looked up and just stood there, his eyes as big as saucers. He just stood there looking at Susie in all her glory, mesmerized, like a deer in headlights."

"Betty said he snapped out of it as soon as he heard his name being yelled—only to see Grandma hurdling the fire and running at him. He turned right around and started running for his very life."

"So, anyway, I rounded the bend in the track just in time to see Susie tackle George and then Bill, being chased by your Grandma, trip, and fall right on top of George and Susie and her two socks."

By this time, the old man was laughing so hard he could hardly breathe.

"But here is the funny part..." The old man said, gasping for breath. "Your Grandma was so close behind Bill, she didn't see the pileup and didn't have time to stop. As Bill trips, she follows him to the ground. Her dress flies up over her head - and here is the thing, the thing is, SHE DIDN'T HAVE ANY PANTIES ON!"

He rocks so far back in his chair, roaring with laughter, the boy thought he was going to tip it over, and across the lake the fancy neighbor stomped out onto his dock to investigate the racket.

The boy jumped to his feet, howling with laughter. "MY GRANDMA!?"

Crying and breathing hard, Granddad squeaks out:

"Apparently she had sat in some water earlier, and she was drying her panties over the fire as well." He fights to catch his breath, 40 years of memories floating in the way. Anyway, I come around the corner, and this is what I see.... George is on his back; Susie is face down on George; Bill is on HIS back, lying on top of Susie, and Grandma's hiney is shining in the moonlight!"

The old man's chair slowed as he stared out into memory,

muttering to himself with a knowing grin, "That woman had such a nice arse."

Then he sighed, straightened himself in his chair and, with words laced with false chivalry, launched back into the story.

"Well, I did the only thing a real man would do to protect his woman's honor. I raced straight over to the pile, straddled them all, and lifted your Grandma's dress up to try and cover her butt. At that exact moment, Betty comes trotting down the path."

"So here I am holding up Grandma's dress, like I am looking at her bum, while Grandma is screaming and slapping Bill; while Susie is flapping like a fish, waving a couple of wet socks screaming, 'Don't look! Don't look!' And George all this time is wiggling his arms and legs trying to get out from all of it... and then Betty... Betty, she falls to the ground, laughing so hard she starts screaming, 'Stop, I'm peeing myself, I'm peeing myself.'"

He can't help himself and starts rocking and roaring again. "What a delightful mess that night was!"

As a soft afternoon breeze picks up, a quiet smile replaces the raucous laughter, and he wipes his eyes. His gaze shifts beyond the lake and he starts mumbles again to himself. "We had such fun together; we sure did. For years we told each other that story."

The boy excused himself to make them both iced tea, while Granddad smiled and nodded to memories of his long-passed friends as if they had all gathered for one last retelling of their adventures.

As the condensation dripped down the side of grandma's favorite crystal cut glasses, the old man picked up the story again, but this time it was different; there was a purpose to it.

"As I told you, the river was high and cold, and running fast, but we were never worried. We knew that between the six of us, we could handle anything thrown at us. Jack, we had the right people on the boat. We had packed light, and we had each other. We all had our strengths, and we covered for each other's weaknesses."

"How long did it the trip take you?" the boy asked.

"Two weeks," the old man replied.

The boy screwed up his face. "That doesn't seem right; it's only 300 miles by road. I would think it would have been more like a lazy four days by boat."

"We never took the boat, son. We took the raft," Granddad said, waiting for that revelation to sink in.

The boy pointed down the hill, "You're kidding, that old thing?"

With false dignity, the old man replied, "Well lad, THAT old raft is a little bit like me; she was all that and then some back in the day."

"That's not what I mean, Granddad. Why didn't you just take the speedboat?"

"Between here and Lewisville are two sets of rapids. Between Lewisville and the coast, is another four. The only way to get a boat down the rapids is to go around them. If the rapids were too rough or difficult, you have to paddle a shore, unpack the boat, carry everything up the riverbank and through the bush, and back down to below the rapids. We would then have to repack it all before heading off again. All that takes time and some doing, and you can't do it in a speedboat. "

The young man shook his head. "That sounds like a lot of effort."

The old man lit his pipe and reflected, "Life takes a lot of effort, son. Getting to where you are supposed to get takes some doing."

As the smoke bellowed around them, the boy breathed in the memories of his childhood, as his granddad continued. "There are two types of people in this world—there are raft people, and there are speedboat people—and one day you are going to have to choose which one of those you are going to be."

Without hesitation, the young man said, "I'll take that speedboat any day."

Knowingly, the old man chuckled, "At 20, we all do. I know I certainly did. Right up to that trip down the river to the coast at Clarkestown."

The boy asked, "What happened?"

"Nothing happened. I just realized something on that trip, and it changed everything for me. It changed the way I loved your Grandma, it changed the way I did life."

The old man stood to his feet and said, "Come walk with me."

As they meandered back down to the dock, he continued to muse. "Before the Clarkstown trip, I was a speedboat guy just like you and just like your dad. Always running hard, always charging full steam ahead. Every weekend, I would get out on the lake and tear it up, racing from one end to the other as fast as I could. Every summer, Grandma and

I would pack all the kids up and I would trailer the boat down to the coast, where we would race it around some more. I felt great being the 'Captain' of the speedboat. I never thought about the current or the direction of the water. I had all the power; I was in charge. I loved it."

The old man pointed out over the lake with the stem of his pipe. "As long as this lake was clear, and I had enough fuel, and there were no obstacles in my way, and the weather was perfect, I could go as fast as I wanted to from here to over there by old Ray's place and back again."

"BUT—and it's a big one—that was as far as I could go. My surroundings limited me. Fuel limited me. And I was limiting everybody else as well. Because in the speedboat, there was only one person giving input into the direction, me; everyone else just sat there disengaged from the journey, sitting there sightseeing. We might have been in the boat together, but we weren't in the adventure together."

He climbed down the ladder and motioned the young

23

man into the old raft; they cast off, and rowed towards the middle of the lake where they sat side by side, enveloped by the comfortable silence that comes with a shared life.

Granddad looked up as a hawk screeched, circled lazily overhead before flying South. He turned to the boy and said, "After we got back to the campsite, Susie went off to get changed. The rest of us just sat there, embarrassed and not sure if we should laugh or cry. Then Susie walked up to us real awkward-like, looked at each of us and softly said, 'I'd appreciate it if we never talked about this again.'"

"Billy gallantly stood up and walked towards her and put his arms around her, and with a completely straight face, very lovingly said, 'I totally agree with my fiancé, Susie. We shall never speak of this again. However, if we ever did, I would have to say is that they are the greatest set of—'"

"Susie looked at him, horrified, and said in her best Sunday-school-teacher-voice, 'William Thomas!'"

"Billy smiled wide and added, '.... EYES that I have ever

seen, and I plan to be looking at them and talking about them for the rest of my life.' It was about 20 minutes before we stopped laughing."

The old man stretched an old protesting knee straight and ventured to the heart of the matter. "At that moment, I decided I wanted to have people around me I could share my life with. Not just the good bits, but the awkward and embarrassing bits as well."

"I realized how lonely I was and how hard I worked trying to make life happen on my own. I was keeping everyone at arm's length, even your Grandma, just in case they slowed me down."

"You see, Jack, with a speedboat, we could never have gotten to the coast. We would have probably cracked the hull on the first rapid. People might have gotten hurt, maybe even thrown overboard or even drowned. If we had made it over the first rapid without smashing the hull, at some point we would have run out of fuel." He reached out and patted his grandson on the shoulder. "I might have been the sole captain of the boat, but what is the use of being the captain of a sinking ship or a ship that's going nowhere?"

As they rowed back towards the shore, he continued, "Being on the raft was different; we were all in this together. As a group, we decided what gear we needed for the trip. We all rowed together, pulling towards a common goal, yet all the time we were going with the flow of the river, following the current. It's not like we didn't have control; we just trusted that the river knew where it was going, and we weren't trying to fight it by rowing in the opposite direction."

"If we hit a difficulty, a challenge, like rapids, we all had input as to whether or not we thought we could make it. If we didn't think we could, we all got involved in carrying our gear and the raft up and over to the other side. Together we did the hard work, and together we enjoyed the reward of drifting with the current as well."

The warm glow of the afternoon sun washed over them reassuringly as they pottered around on the dock, putting everything back, ready for the next time they would need it. Granddad, in an uncustomary act of intimacy, pulled the young man to himself. He kissed him on the cheek and held him long enough for the awkwardness of rare physical affection to fade.

Granddad stood back and said, "Jack, your daddy was a special man, one of those rare combinations of both big dreamer and passionate doer. The one regret I have is that I never got to tell him about my trip down the river and my thoughts on the raft and the speedboat. Your daddy never stopped long enough to hear me, and I never made a point of sharing it. Then one day it was too late."

He then turned and looked down at the speedboat bobbing silently in the water. "I sometimes wonder if I had made him listen, maybe he would have slowed down long enough to take a holiday, and maybe he would never have died like he did."

"You shouldn't say that, Granddad, that's not fair to you."

The old man shook his head, "This isn't a pity party, son. I stopped throwing those years ago. Besides, there is no room on the raft for extra baggage. No, this isn't extra baggage;

this is my one bag. This is the one thing I have carried all these years." Through silent tears, the old man said "And today I give it to you. I want to give you this story. It is the gift I wanted to give to your Dad, but now I give it to you."

He turned them both towards the house, the golden glow of sunset filling the air with a stillness beyond what they saw.

"At some point in his/her life, every person will face the same choice I did. Will they limit themselves to being the captain of a speedboat, or will they take a chance on faith and love, a risk on their friends and family? With everything that's in me, I pray you will be the sort of man who trusts that God Himself knows where the river of your life is destined to flow, and that you will choose to row with Him and not against Him."

AUTHOR'S PERSONAL REMARKS

This is not the life I would have planned for or wanted for myself, but it is the life I have been given, and I am grateful for it. Instead of being ashamed of it or scared by it, I have come to accept it and love it as my own.

I have my best friend at my side, my life partner, someone more than capable of pulling an oar and sharing the load. And I trust that this river that is our adventure will take us to where we are supposed to go.

Melissa and I hope and pray that those of you who have been through the worst of it, will allow it to bring out the best in you.

We wish you Peace and Much Grace for the journey ahead.

Relax, you're going to make it.

John and Melissa

ARTISTS/CONTRIBUTORS

Dr. John A. King, Author

I like to smoke cigars and sit by myself--that's why I took up writing.

Melissa King, Contributor, Layout Designer

Many artists down through history talk of a "muse" that propelled them to greatness--complex, fun loving, inspiring. I have the privilege of having breakfast with mine daily.

Ricardo Ayala, Artist

Ricardo continues to bring our words to life for us. We couldn't have done this project without him.

To see more of Ricardo's amazing work, find him (like I did) on IG @unoriginal_doodler.

Also by Dr. John A. King

DR. JOHN A. KING

#DEALWITHIT
LIVING WELL WITH PTSD

"The book is a well written, highly entertaining and informative guide that ANYONE can use to improve their life. it doesn't matter if you're suffering from PTSD, addiction or you just want to be successful. The principles behind John's plan to become the best he can be apply to EVERYONE who wants to be the best version of themselves..."

ANDREW CURTISS - U.S. Army Special Forces Veteran & Author of *1984 Redux*

This book shares John's gritty process of rebuilding his life after the onset of Complex Post Traumatic Stress. On his journey, you'll find practical tools, unlikely mentors and his trademark Aussie sarcasm. #dealwithit is the perfect book for anyone who is getting up to go again, or is in the middle of the fight and just needs to hear, "You can make it."

Visit drjohnaking.com/shop to purchase.

No Working Title: a Life in Progress is a collection of poetry, writings, stories and art that deal with the taboo topic of the effects of sexual abuse and pornography on boys as they grow into men.

**This is an adult book that deals with adult concepts in adult language.

Visit drjohnaking.com/shop to purchase.

NO WORKING TITLE
A LIFE IN PROGRESS

by Dr. John A. King

Exploring the effects of sexual abuse and pornography on boys as they grow to manhood.

www.ingramcontent.com/pod-product-compliance
Lightning Source LLC
Chambersburg PA
CBHW080905120626
46555CB00008B/2967